GLORIA ESTEFAN

A Real-Life Reader Biography

Sue Boulais

Mitchell Lane Publishers, Inc.
P.O. Box 200 • Childs, Maryland 21916

Copyright © 1998 by Mitchell Lane Publishers. All rights reserved. No part of this book may be reproduced without written permission from the publisher. Printed and bound in the United States of America.

First Printing

Real-Life Reader Biographies

Selena	Robert Rodriguez	Mariah Carey	Rafael Palmeiro
Tommy Nuñez	Trent Dimas	Cristina Saralegui	Andres Galarraga
Oscar De La Hoya	**Gloria Estefan**	Jimmy Smits	Mary Joe Fernandez
Cesar Chavez	Isabel Allende	Vanessa Williams	Sinbad
Bob Vila	Raul Julia	Paula Abdul	Chuck Norris

Library of Congress Cataloging-in-Publication Data
Boulais, Sue.
    Gloria Estefan / Sue Boulais.
        p. cm. — (A real-life reader biography)
    Includes index.
    Summary: Presents a biography of the Cuban-born singer and composer who has recorded such hits as "Into the Light," "Conga," and "Reach."
    ISBN 1-883845-62-9 (lib. bnd.)
    1. Estefan, Gloria—Juvenile literature. 2. Singers—United States—Biography—Juvenile literature. [1. Estefan, Gloria. 2. Singers. 3. Cuban Americans—Biography. 4. Women—Biography.] I. Title. II. Series.
ML3930.E85B68 1997
782.42164'092—dc21   97-42783
[B]   CIP
                                                                                                                    AC MN

ABOUT THE AUTHOR: Sue Boulais is a freelance writer/editor based in Orlando, Florida. She has published numerous books, including **Famous Astronauts** (Media Materials) and **Hispanic American Achievers** (Frog Publications). Previously, she served as an editor for *Weekly Reader* and Harcourt Brace.

PHOTO CREDITS: cover: AP Photo/Anders Krus Berg; p. 4 sketch by Barbara Tidman; p. 12 Shooting Star/Raul de Molina; p. 16 AP Photo; p. 18 courtesy Estefan Enterprises; p. 23 AP Photo; p. 26 Bettmann; p. 28 Globe Photos/Fitzroy Barrett

ACKNOWLEDGMENTS: The following story has been thoroughly researched and checked for accuracy. To the best of our knowledge, it represents a true story. Though we attempt to contact each person profiled in our Real-Life Reader Biographies, for various reasons, we were unable to authorize every story.

Table of Contents

Chapter 1   Escaping with Music 5

Chapter 2   Making Music with Emilio 10

Chapter 3   Changes 15

Chapter 4   World Fame—and Tragedy 20

Chapter 5   "Here for Each Other" 27

Chronology 31

Selected Discography 32

Index 32

Chapter 1
Escaping with Music

Gloria Estefan was born Gloria Maria Fajardo on September 1, 1957. She was the first child born to Gloria and José Manuel Fajardo. She has a younger sister, Rebecca (Becky). For about the first year and a half of her life, Gloria lived with her family in Havana, Cuba. Her mother taught kindergarten there. Her father was an officer in the Cuban army.

In 1959, however, a war began in Cuba, and many Cubans fled to

Gloria Fajardo was born in Havana, Cuba.

When Gloria was two years old, her family fled Cuba and settled in Miami, Florida.

the United States for safety. These people were called refugees. The Fajardos were among the refugees. By the time Gloria was two years old, José Fajardo had settled the family in Miami, Florida. He then went back to Cuba to fight against Fidel Castro, who had taken control of the government.

Other Cuban men in Florida had also gone back to Cuba to fight. Many, including José, were captured and kept in a Cuban prison for nearly two years. Gloria and her mother were alone in the United States. The U.S. government tried to help get the prisoners back to the United States. Finally, just a few days before Christmas in 1962, José Fajardo was freed. He returned to Miami.

Life in the United States wasn't easy for the family. The Fajardos spoke only Spanish. Many Americans didn't want Cuban refugees in the United States. They treated the refugees badly.

But Gloria was determined to succeed. At school she quickly learned English and caught up with the other children. She was always at the head of her class, even when her home life became very difficult.

When Gloria's father came back from Cuba, he joined the U.S. Army. In 1966, when war began between the United States and Vietnam, José Fajardo volunteered for duty. He served in Vietnam for two years.

Gloria was ten when her father came home. The girls and their mother knew something was wrong with him. Even though he had not been hurt in the fighting, Gloria says, "He'd fall for no reason."

> **Life wasn't easy in the United States. At the time, the Fajardos spoke only Spanish.**

Gloria's father got sick and she had to take care of him. Her mother had to go to work to support the family.

Her father was told he had multiple sclerosis. This disease can cause many kinds of problems because it attacks the nerves. In just a few months, her father could not walk. Mrs. Fajardo went back to work to support the family. She also went back to college and got an American teaching degree. Then she taught public school in Miami.

Gloria helped out at home as much as she could. She became a little mother to her family. From the age of 11 until she was 16, Gloria took care of her sister, Becky, and her father.

José Fajardo needed constant care. "It was around the clock," says Gloria. "It wasn't easy. His mind went before his body. There were times when he wasn't aware of who I was, or who any of us were. It was very hard."

During those years, music became very important to Gloria. She remembers, "When my father was ill, music was my escape. I'd lock myself up in my room with my guitar."

In her room, Gloria would listen to music for hours and hours. She loved to sing along with the ballads and pop songs. She learned to play the guitar. Soon she could play along with her favorite songs.

In her room, Gloria would listen to music for hours and hours.

Chapter 2
Making Music with Emilio

Music became more and more important to Gloria as she went through her teen years. During her senior year in high school, she and some friends put together a band to play for a party.

The father of another band member knew Emilio Estefan, a popular band leader in Miami. The father invited Emilio to one of the girls' rehearsals, to give the girls a few tips.

Music became very important to Gloria.

Gloria met Emilio again three months after that first meeting. She says, "My mother dragged me to this wedding that I really didn't want to go to, and Emilio's band was playing. Emilio remembered me and asked me to sing a song with the band." A few weeks after that, Emilio asked Gloria to join the band permanently.

At first, Gloria said no. She had just begun classes at the University of Miami. Because her high school grades were so good—she made honor roll every semester—Gloria had received a scholarship.

She had never thought about joining a band or following a full-time musical career. Of course, she loved music and liked to sing, but mostly for fun. She worried that if she joined Emilio's band, she would not have enough time for her

Emilio Estefan asked Gloria to join his band.

studies. Gloria's mother worried, too.

But Emilio promised Gloria that she would perform only on weekends and vacations. Her mother agreed that Gloria could sing, but only if Gloria agreed to finish college. Gloria promised, then accepted Emilio's offer. "I loved music so much that I couldn't let a great opportunity like this pass me by," she says.

With Gloria as lead singer, the band had a better, different, very special sound.

Gloria and Emilio were married in 1978.

Soon, Emilio changed the band's name from the Miami Latin Boys to Miami Sound Machine. "All of a sudden," Gloria says, "I was going to parties every weekend, singing with the whole band behind me." She loved to perform and came to realize that music was her calling.

Through their music, Gloria and Emilio got to know each other. Like the Fajardos, Emilio and his family had come from Cuba. Like many Cuban refugees, they had settled in Miami. They were very poor when they arrived in the United States, so Emilio worked at many jobs to help support the family. By the time he met Gloria, Emilio was the director of marketing at Bacardi Imports.

But Emilio's real passion was music, and his part-time band was one of the most popular dance

Through their music, Gloria and Emilio got to know each other.

> **Gloria sang with the band for a while before Emilio asked her out.**

bands in Miami. By the time Gloria joined the band, Emilio had long been thinking about quitting his job with Bacardi and working with his band full time.

Gloria sang with the band for a year and a half before Emilio asked her out. They fell in love, dating steadily during Gloria's last two years at the university. In May 1978, Gloria graduated from college. Three months later, on September 1, 1978, she married Emilio.

Chapter 3
Changes

After their marriage, Gloria and Emilio began a long, hard job—getting the band known all over the world. The Miami Sound Machine's first album, *Renacer* (1978), was a collection of disco, pop, and original ballads sung in Spanish. During the next two years, the band released two more albums. All the albums sold well in Miami, but they didn't get much attention anywhere else.

In 1980, two changes took place in Gloria's family. Her father died

The Miami Sound Machine released their first album in 1978.

In 1980, Emilio and Gloria had a son. They named him Nayib.

after twelve years of crippling illness. He had been in a Veteran's Administration Hospital since 1975. His long illness had brought the family much grief. Gloria says, "It just gets to the point where you pray that the suffering will end, because you can't imagine why anyone has to go through something like that."

That same year, though, Gloria and Emilio's first child was born, bringing much joy and happiness to the family. The couple named the boy Nayib. They decided at once that their son was the most important thing in their lives.

Not long after Nayib was born, Emilio quit his full-time job. He wanted to give all of his attention to making a success of Gloria and the Miami Sound Machine.

Gloria is an enthusiastic performer.

Soon the group signed a contract with Discos CBS International, the Miami-based

Hispanic division of CBS Records. Discos CBS International specializes in Latin music. Company officials decided that the Miami Sound Machine should only release albums in Spanish. The band's recordings would be sold in the Latin American countries, where the people speak mostly Spanish.

The Miami Sound Machine originally released songs in Spanish for the Latin American market.

Gloria explains: "CBS thought we would sell better in Latin America if we sang in Spanish. But we kept the right to record in English, because eventually we wanted to try for the States."

During the next several years, Miami Sound Machine recorded four

Spanish-language albums. From those albums came a dozen songs that became worldwide hits. By 1984, Miami Sound Machine was one of the most popular recording groups in Latin America. And—even better—Gloria Estefan and the Miami Sound Machine were becoming popular all over the world.

By 1984, the Miami Sound Machine was a popular group.

Chapter 4
World Fame—
and Tragedy

In the 1980s the Miami Sound Machine began to record English-language songs.

Throughout the rest of the 1980s, Gloria and the Miami Sound Machine recorded song after song. Each was a bigger success than the one before. During those years, too, the group began to record English-language songs.

The string of hits began with "Dr. Beat" (1984), a Latin-style dance song that the group recorded in English. "Dr. Beat" was on the record's B side, the side that usually gets no air time on radio. But it wasn't long before "Dr. Beat" could be heard on many Miami radio stations, both Spanish and English-language. When CBS released it nationally as a dance single, it zoomed to number ten on the dance charts.

In 1984 the group also recorded the album *Eyes of Innocence*; *Primitive Love* came out the next year. These two albums made Gloria and the Miami Sound Machine a success all over English-speaking America. In fact, "Conga," a single from *Primitive Love,* went to number two on the American pop charts. The song also made *Billboard*'s dance, Latin, and Black charts—the first song in American music history to appear on four charts at the same time.

Their first English-language hit was "Dr. Beat."

In 1990, Gloria performed at the American Music Awards and the Grammy Awards ceremonies.

Let It Loose (1987) stayed on the pop charts for more than two years. The album sold three million copies in the United States alone, and it produced four top ten hits. The group performed at the closing of the 1988 Pan American Games—even though the Cuban government protested because it wanted a Latin-American band to play. And, in 1989, *Cuts Both Ways* demonstrated Gloria's talent as a songwriter. The album contained ten of the many songs she had written during a 20-month tour.

The early months of 1990 carried on the streak of success. Gloria and the band performed at the American Music Awards and the Grammy Awards ceremonies. From CBS, they received the Crystal Globe award, a prize that goes to performers who sell more than 5 million records outside their own country. Gloria met President George Bush at the White House, where he honored her for her drug prevention work with teenagers. Life shined brightly for Gloria, her family, and the band.

But on March 20—the day after she visited the White House—tragedy struck.

On March 19, 1990, Gloria was a guest at the White House. She was honored by President George Bush. Her son, Nayib, and husband, Emilio, were with her.

When it was time to go to their next concert, they had to go through a snow-storm.

Headed for their next concert in Syracuse, New York, Gloria, Emilio, and Nayib were traveling through a snowstorm. Near the Pennsylvania–New York state line, a tractor trailer had jackknifed across the road and was blocking traffic. As Gloria's tour bus came to a stop, it was hit from behind. The tour bus was pushed into a truck that was stopped ahead of it on the road. The front of the bus caved in, and all three family members were thrown to the bus floor.

Emilio was not seriously hurt. He found Nayib lying under a mountain of purses, books, and bags with a broken collarbone.

Gloria was relieved that her husband and son were alive. But she was in terrible pain. She had been thrown from the couch on which she had been lying, and she could not move. For more than an hour, Gloria lay waiting for a police helicopter. She didn't want Nayib to know how much pain she was in. "I was forced to really keep a lot of control," Gloria remembers, "because I didn't want him to feel that we had lost that grip for him, so he helped me hang on."

When Gloria finally arrived at the hospital in Scranton, the doctors told her what she had suspected: her back was broken. Gloria thought her career as a performer was over.

Flown to the Hospital for Joint Diseases in New York City, she underwent a new and very risky kind of surgery on March 23. If the operation failed, she would be paralyzed forever.

Their bus was in an accident. Gloria broke her back. She thought her career was over.

When Gloria's back had healed, she went on tour for her Into the Light *album.*

The operation was a complete success. However, complete recovery was another matter. It took many months of rest and therapy.

Thousands of cards and letters from fans all over the country brought good wishes and support to Gloria. That support helped her through the long months of recovery. By January 1991, Gloria was performing again.

Chapter 5
"Here for Each Other"

Since the accident, Gloria has had many more successes. She and the Miami Sound Machine keep turning out hit albums. They perform for world leaders and at important events. And Gloria keeps piling up honors and awards. She is most proud of her Ellis Island Congressional Medal of Honor. The medal makes her a representative for all Americans when she travels. She also represents the millions of Hispanics who, like her family,

Gloria is most proud of her Ellis Island Congressional Medal of Honor.

make their homes in the United States.

In 1994, there was more good news for Gloria and Emilio. They became parents again when Emily Marie Estefan Fajardo was born on December 5. Emily was a dream come true for the Estefans. Before the bus accident, they had talked about another baby. But, after the accident, no one was sure that Gloria would be able to have another child.

Gloria is also a passionate, tireless worker for those with troubles. People throughout Miami

Gloria with Emilio and baby Emily.

call her "a star with a heart." When Hurricane Andrew roared through Miami, she wrote and recorded the song "Always Tomorrow." The song brought nearly $3 million to Gloria and Emilio—all of which they gave to the people who lost their homes and loved ones to Hurricane Andrew.

For many years, Gloria has also worked hard to help battered and abused children in Miami. "I've seen things that have ruined the lives of children," she says.

"The children in our care are fortunate that Gloria and Emilio have both given so much of themselves," says Dr. Mary Louise Cole of the Children's Home Society of Florida. Laurie Kay, the Society's Director of Development, gives Gloria credit for the very existence of Children's Home

Gloria and Emilio raised money for the victims of Hurricane Andrew.

Society. "Gloria and her husband have done wonders for us," she says. "I wish there were more Gloria Estefans."

To be with her own children, Gloria has turned down several offers for movie roles. "Right now, I just want to concentrate on my children and watch them grow up into happy, healthy adults," she states. She tries to see to it that their home on one of Miami Beach's islands is always filled with fun and friends.

Gloria is ever thankful she was able to recover from her accident and return to the performing she loves. "I was always a thankful person," she says, "because I did go through some difficult things, but you tend to forget and get caught up in petty stuff. The bottom line is that we're here for each other."

> "The bottom line is that we're here for each other."

Chronology

- Born September 1, 1957, in Havana, Cuba; mother: Gloria Fajardo; father: José Manuel Fajardo
- 1959, family left Cuba; settled in Miami, Florida
- Father returned from Vietnam with an illness that caused many problems
- 1975, joined Emilio Estefan's band, the Miami Latin Boys; band changed name to Miami Sound Machine (MSM)
- September 1, 1978, married Emilio Estefan
- 1978, MSM released first album, *Renacer*
- 1981, signed with Discos CBS International to record Spanish-language albums
- 1982, "Dr. Beat" climbed to number ten on the dance charts
- 1984, *Eyes of Innocence,* first English-language album
- 1985, *Primitive Love,* first successful U. S. English-language album
- 1987, *Let It Loose*; album stayed on charts for two years
- 1989, *Cuts Both Ways*; album established Gloria as a talented songwriter
- 1990, MSM performed at the American Music Awards and the Grammy Awards ceremonies; earned Crystal Globe Award
- March 20, 1990, Gloria's back was broken in a bus accident
- 1991, Gloria returned to performing; MSM releases *Into the Light*
- 1992, *Greatest Hits*; B'nai B'rith named Gloria Humanitarian of the Year; Hispanic magazine *Vista* voted Gloria Hispanic Woman of the Year
- 1993, *Mi Tierra*, an all-Spanish tribute to their homeland; Gloria received Ellis Island Congressional Medal of Honor; awarded star on Hollywood Walk of Fame
- 1995, *Abrienda Puertas*; gave concert in Cuba; performed for Pope John Paul II; performed for President Bill Clinton and First Lady
- 1996, *Destiny,* first English-language album since 1991; performed at Olympics in Atlanta, Georgia
- 1997, *Destiny* certified platinum

Selected Discography

Renacer	Discos CBS International	1981
Otra Vez	Discos CBS International	1981
Rio	Discos CBS International	1982
Eyes of Innocence	Epic Records	1984
Primitive Love	Epic Records	1985
Let It Loose	Epic Records	1987
Cuts Both Ways	Epic Records	1989
Into the Light	Epic Records	1991
Greatest Hits	Epic Records	1992
Mi Tierra	Epic Records	1993
Abriendo Puertas	Epic Records	1995
Destiny	Epic Records	1996

Index

albums 15, 18–19, 21–22, 26, 27, 32
American Music Awards 22
back surgery 25–26
birth of 5
bus accident 24–25, 30
Bush, George 23
Castro, Fidel 6
charitable work of 28–30
"Conga" 21
Crystal Globe Award 22
Cuba 5, 6, 7, 13, 22
Discos CBS International 17–18, 21, 22
"Dr. Beat" 20–21
education of 11–12, 14
Ellis Island Congressional Medal of Honor 27
Estefan, Emilio 10, 11–14, 15, 16, 24, 28, 29
Estefan, Emily (daughter) 28, 30
Estefan, Nayib (son) 16, 23, 24–25, 30
Grammy Awards 22
Hurricane Andrew 29
marriage of 14
Miami Sound Machine 13, 15, 16, 18–19, 20–22, 27
parents of 5, 6–9, 15–16

3 1911 00356 6313

```
J           Boulais, Sue.
B
Estefan     Gloria Estefan.
B
```

BEGINNING READERS

DATE			
21-5/18			

HICKSVILLE PUBLIC LIBRARY
169 JERUSALEM AVENUE
HICKSVILLE, NY 11801

BAKER & TAYLOR